Welcome to ALA

If you are looking for fast, fun-to-read stories with colorful characters, lots of kid-friendly humor, easy-to-follow action, entertaining story lines, and lively illustrations, then **ALADDIN QUIX** is for you!

But wait, there's more!

If you're also looking for stories with tables of contents; word lists; about-the-book questions; 64, 80, or 96 pages; short chapters; short paragraphs; and large fonts, then **ALADDIN QUIX** is *definitely* for you!

ALADDIN QUIX: The next step between ready to reads and longer, more challenging chapter books, for readers five to eight years old.

**Read the other books
in the Elf Academy series!**

Trouble in Toyland
Reindeer Games
Happy Santa Day!

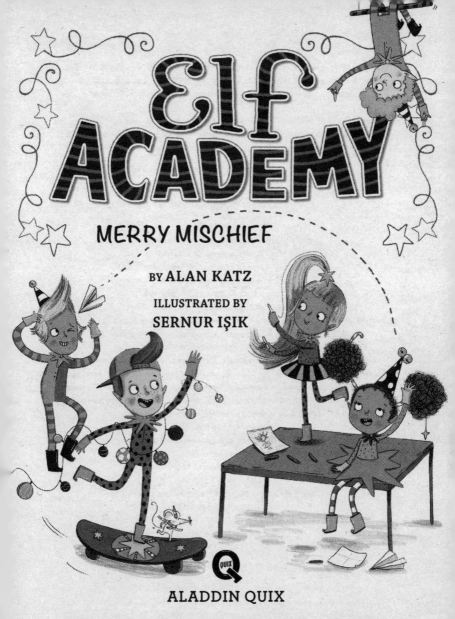

ELF ACADEMY

MERRY MISCHIEF

BY ALAN KATZ

ILLUSTRATED BY
SERNUR IŞIK

ALADDIN QUIX

NEW YORK LONDON TORONTO SYDNEY NEW DELHI

ALADDIN QUIX

Simon & Schuster Children's Publishing Division

1230 Avenue of the Americas, New York, New York 10020

First Aladdin QUIX paperback edition September 2023

Text copyright © 2023 by Simon & Schuster, Inc.

Illustrations copyright © 2023 by Sernur Işik

Also available in an Aladdin QUIX hardcover edition.

All rights reserved, including the right of reproduction in whole or in part in any form.

ALADDIN and the related marks and colophon are registered trademarks of Simon & Schuster, Inc.

For information about special discounts for bulk purchases, please contact Simon & Schuster Special Sales at 1-866-506-1949 or business@simonandschuster.com.

The Simon & Schuster Speakers Bureau can bring authors to your live event. For more information or to book an event contact the Simon & Schuster Speakers Bureau at 1-866-248-3049 or visit our website at www.simonspeakers.com.

Designed by Tiara Iandiorio

The illustrations for this book were rendered digitally.

The text of this book was set in Archer Medium.

Manufactured in the United States of America 0723 OFF

2 4 6 8 10 9 7 5 3 1

Library of Congress Control Number 2023933149

ISBN 9781534467989 (hc)

ISBN 9781534467972 (pbk)

ISBN 9781534467996 (ebook)

To Craig—welcome to the family!
—A. K.

Cast of Characters

Andy Snowden: An Elf Academy student

Ms. Allspice: Reindeer riding teacher

Mr. Yardley: Comet counting teacher

Annie Bellows: Youngest elf at Elf Academy

Ziggy Miller: An Elf Academy student

Assistant Principal Winterfield: Assistant principal at Elf Academy

Ms. Dow: The toy workshop teacher at Elf Academy

Jay: Andy's best friend

Jane: Ms. Dow's niece

Trevor: Ms. Dow's nephew

Susu: Andy's twin sister

Nicole: Susu's best friend

Craig: Andy and Susu's older brother

Principal Evergreen: Principal of Elf Academy

Kal: An Elf Academy student

Zahara: An Elf Academy student

CONTENTS

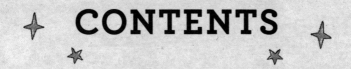

1

The Favor

Andy Snowden knew just about everything about everyone at Elf Academy.

He knew that **Ms. Allspice** taught reindeer riding and that **Mr. Yardley** taught comet counting,

1

that little **Annie Bellows** was the youngest elf at school, that **Ziggy Miller** had just celebrated his ninth birthday, and that peppermint-chocolate potato chips were **Assistant Principal Winterfield**'s favorite snack.

There wasn't much that **escaped** Andy's eagle eyes.

So when he walked into his classroom on a snowy Monday morning and saw two elves he had never seen before sitting in the first two desks, he thought

he was in the wrong place.

"Andy Snowden! Just the elf I wanted to see. Please come to my desk," said his teacher, **Ms. Dow.**

Uh-oh, Andy thought. *Am I in trouble already? How can that be possible? School just started!*

He wished he could jump onto the tail of a shooting star and fly home.

But a shooting star wasn't going to help Andy. As he walked to the front of the classroom, he looked at his best friend, **Jay**.

"Good luck," Jay whispered.

"Ms. Dow, before you say anything, I did the science homework, and I am almost done building the puppy palace, and I straightened up the ribbon room before I left Friday, and—"

"Thank you, Andy," Ms. Dow said. "But that's *not* why I want to see you. I would like to ask you a **favor**."

Andy breathed a sigh of **relief**.

"Sure, Ms. Dow. Anything you need. I'm great at favors. I'll do whatever you want!"

Ms. Dow smiled.

"Did you notice anything new or different when you arrived this morning?" she asked.

Oh no. **A quiz!** Andy thought. But then he remembered. Now Andy was the one who smiled and said, "Two new students?"

"That's right, Andy. My niece **Jane** and her brother **Trevor** have just moved to the North Pole," Ms. Dow explained. "And since you are such a friendly and **knowledgeable** elf, I could use

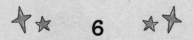

your help in introducing them to your friends, teaching them all about Elf Academy, and making them feel welcome."

Andy turned around and looked at Jane and Trevor. He waved to them and smiled, and they waved back shyly. Then they joined him and Ms. Dow at the front of the room.

"Jane and Trevor, would you like to say anything to the class?" Ms. Dow asked.

"Um, well," Jane began.

"First I want to learn how to make bubble machines. Then I'd like to study the reindeer rides," she said.

"And I want to be able to make the best and biggest snow creatures," Trevor added. "There's so much to know that I'm not really sure where to begin."

Ms. Dow smiled warmly at her niece and nephew. "Now back to your seats. Before we start our Majestic Mountains lesson, I want to **remind** you all that I will

be choosing an Elf of the Week by Friday. You never know who it will be, so stay on your toes."

Andy knew it must be hard to be the new elves in town.

★ ★   9   ★ ★

I can't do this alone, he thought. *I'd better ask Jay, Susu, and Nicole to help me. We'll make sure the North Pole feels like home to Jane and Trevor right away.*

2

Two Tricksters

Even though Andy liked going to school every morning, his favorite time of day was when Elf Academy was over. Walking home with his friends, or his older brother, **Craig**, or his twin sister, Susu, Andy didn't have to worry or think about homework or pop quizzes or eating yucky lima beans for dinner. He could:

- Tell jokes:

"What did the snow women eat for breakfast?

"Snowflakes!"

- Play freeze tag:

"Jay, you can move now."

- Search for snowdrops:

"Look! Mom's favorite winter flower."

So when Jay said, "Let's ask

Trevor and Jane to walk home with us," it seemed like an elf-tastic idea to make them feel welcome. After the last bell rang, the four elves met at the Elf Academy front entrance and started the trip home.

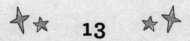

"On the way, Jay and I can show you how to make the perfect snow creatures—tigers, penguins, you name it," Andy said to Trevor and Jane.

"You have to start from the beginning with the snowball," Jay added. "All elves know that the snow has to be **powdery**—not too dry or too wet. And gloves help so that your hands don't get too cold as you pack the snow into a firm, round shape."

Andy continued, "It will take a

lot of work before you get the hang of it, but as you can see, snow is everywhere you look, so you can practice anytime you want. Do you have any questions before we begin?" he asked.

There was silence.

"Trevor? Jane?" Andy said.

And then Andy and Jay realized that Ms. Dow's niece and nephew weren't behind them anymore.

"Jay! **We've lost them!**" Andy cried. "On the first day! Ms. Dow is going to have our heads, especially mine! I was supposed to make sure they were having a good time, not a *goodbye* time!"

Andy was so worried, he almost didn't hear when his name was called.

"Hey, Andy! Hey, Jay! Looking for us?" Jane called out.

The best friends quickly turned, and

Zip!

Zip!

Zap!

Snowball after perfectly round snowball came from every direction, smacking Andy's and Jay's arms, ears, and caps.

Andy was so surprised, he froze in his tracks. But being the five-time

Annual Snowball Fight champ, he quickly **recovered** and started firing snowballs back.

Jay yelled, "Hey! I thought you didn't know anything about snowballs. **You tricked us!**"

"We did, didn't we?" Trevor said, laughing.

"Uh, okay," Andy answered, placing his soaking wet cap back on his head just as they reached his house.

"Thanks so much for a snowtacular afternoon. Our aunt will

be so happy for us," Jane said as they waved goodbye.

"See you tomorrow, everyone," Jay answered.

Andy was finishing up his homework when Susu came into his room.

"How was showing Trevor and Jane around today?" she asked her brother and sat down next to him.

"They had lots of fun," Andy answered. **"Lots!"**

At least I hope those two tricky elves did, he thought.

3

Sweet and Sour

"I bet Trevor and Jane are still going to be **nervous** today," Andy told his brother and sister as they walked to school the next morning. "And we have a double toy-building class. What do you think I should teach them that will make them and Ms. Dow happy?" he asked.

Susu thought for a second. "I can help Jane," she offered. "I'm almost done with my polka-dot dragon chess set. Didn't she say she'd like to make a bubble-blowing machine? Nicole and I made a super bubbly one last year. No problem."

"Great. You and Nicole can work with Jane, and Jay and I will help Trevor with the **basics**, like block building."

Andy nodded as he skipped ahead of his brother and sister. **"See you at school, Susu!"** he shouted. *Maybe Ms. Dow will choose me for Elf of the Week,* Andy thought. *I've never, ever been picked, but maybe being a good friend will help.*

When Andy got to class, Jane and Trevor were already there, but not at their workbenches. He spotted them standing in the back of the room, heads together, whispering.

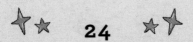

Uh-oh. That looks like trouble, Andy said to himself.

But in the next second he thought, *That's ridiculous. They're probably trying to remember all the other elves' names.*

When Ms. Dow came into the classroom, all the elves quickly sat at their desks.

"Good morning, elves. Before we begin our very busy day, we're going to have a pop quiz on the **fir** trees of North America." She turned to write the quiz questions on the chalkboard.

"Ms. Dow! No!" everyone groaned loudly.

And then a voice called out, "I thought trees were made of bark, Ms. Dow, not fur!" and the entire class started laughing.

Ms. Dow kept writing and answered, "Andy Snowden, that's enough joking. Please see me after the quiz."

Andy couldn't believe his elf ears. Sure, he liked telling jokes and entertaining the class. But today it hadn't been him that had yelled. It had been Trevor! How could Ms. Dow not have recognized Trevor's voice? Maybe it was because of the loud laughter?

And now he was in trouble!

There went his chance at being Elf of the Week. He looked over at Trevor and Jane, who were giggling. They gave Andy a thumbs-up, like it was no big deal.

After the quiz Andy walked up to Ms. Dow's desk.

"I know you wanted to entertain Trevor and Jane, and I appreciate that. However, being **disruptive** before a quiz isn't helpful."

"Ms. Dow, I'm not kidding. It

wasn't . . ." But then Andy stopped trying to explain. *Maybe Trevor was trying to fit in,* he thought.

So Andy said, "I understand.

It won't happen again, ever."

"Thank you, Andy," Ms. Dow replied. "You can go back to your seat."

But the rest of the day was one surprise after another.

The first surprise was at lunch-time. On a table at the front of the cafeteria was a plate of whipped-cream sandwich cookies with a note that said:

Please *TAKE ONE! MADE with CARE by NICOLE.*

Principal Evergreen, who always enjoyed tasting the elves' baking, took a giant bite of the yummy-looking cookie and . . .

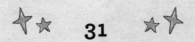

"YUCK!" she shouted, spitting out crumbs. "Nicole, whatever is this made of? It tastes like horseradish and mayonnaise."

Nicole ran up to the principal. "I didn't make these cookies. **Really, I didn't.**"

Andy and Jay glanced across the lunch table and saw Trevor and Jane wink at each other.

The second surprise was after gift-wrapping class. When Ms. Dow opened a beautifully wrapped box from **Kal**, a **slimy** frog jumped out and hopped onto her head.

"Kal, please get this **amphibian** off me. Now!"

"No problem, Ms. Dow, but I didn't give you this! I'm not kidding. I don't even like frogs."

Once again Andy saw Ms. Dow's niece and nephew giggling.

Andy whispered to Jay, "I think they're both up to merry mischief. But why?"

4

Bubbles Everywhere

"Jane, come sit with me," Susu said at the beginning of toy-building class. "I'll show you how to make an awesome bubble maker."

"Thanks, Susu. It's one of my favorite toys," Jane told her.

The elves were super busy all afternoon long.

- Kal was working on sparkly snow mobiles,
- Nicole was painting a robot kangaroo,
- Jay was sewing blue sequins onto a squishy fishy, and

• Andy was putting the finishing touches on a glow-in-the-dark arcade game...

when first one, then three, then eight bubbles floated in front of his face.

The bubble machine must be working, Andy thought.

But before you could say "six slippery sheep on skis," the classroom was filled from floor to ceiling with bubbles! All the newly painted and glittered toys were a bubbly disaster.

Through the bubbles Ms. Dow's

voice boomed, "What is going on here? Susu, is this your Boatload of Bubbles Maker again?"

"No! No, Ms. Dow," Susu answered, **swatting** the bubbles away. "It was . . ." But then she stopped talking. Just like her brother, Susu didn't want to get Jane in trouble, especially with her aunt.

"We'll clean it all up, Ms. Dow. Don't worry," Susu said. "I'm sorry, everyone," she added as her classmates quickly cleaned off their soapy toys and got ready to leave for the day. They couldn't escape the classroom fast enough.

Susu was as angry as Andy could remember ever seeing her. She didn't like being on Ms. Dow's "naughty list," a place Andy knew *very* well. He decided to call an EEM (Emergency Elf Meeting) with Susu, Nicole, Jay, Kal, and **Zahara** so they could figure out what was going on with Jane and Trevor.

"I thought Ms. Dow said Jane

and Trevor wanted to make friends," Zahara said.

"Me too," Jay agreed.

"So why are they blaming *us* for all their tricks?" Susu wondered. "It just doesn't make sense."

A snow flurry started as the group walked home through the woods. The elves were surrounded by towering trees that were now covered with white sprinkles of snow.

Andy was bending down to **scoop** up a handful of flakes when he spotted what looked like a couple of big letters in the middle of the forest.

"Jay," he said. "I don't remember seeing those before, do you? I wonder what they are."

Kal added, "Let's take a closer look. Maybe it's an Elf Academy after-school project?"

But as the kids got closer and closer, they could see a *T* and a *J* made of snow, and then they heard voices that sounded like Trevor's and Jane's.

"I'm sorry we kept tricking all the elves. But we're both so stinky at toy building and baking—and everything! We'd never have made friends once they discovered that we can barely call ourselves elves," Trevor said.

"Shhhhh," Susu whispered as they all listened.

"I know," Jane added. "And maybe Aunt Doris will think about one of us for Elf of the Week instead of Andy, Jay, Susu, Nicole, Kal, or Zahara. They are all, like, super elves. We'll never make friends at Elf Academy if we're not good at something, no matter who our aunt is."

Whoa! Andy thought to himself. *I guess being the new elves in town—and at school—is much harder than I ever would have guessed.*

He **gestured** for the rest of the group to follow him out of the woods.

"EEM part two, at our house, now!" Andy told his friends, and they ran as fast and quietly as their elf feet could carry them to the Snowden house.

5

Merry All Around

"We have to help Jane and Trevor," Jay said.

"They've only been here a few days," Nicole answered. "But I guess we didn't realize how much we've learned at Elf Academy.

I never thought of myself as a super elf," Nicole finished, taking a bite of an apple.

The elves were sitting at the Snowden kitchen table, **munching** on after-school snacks.

"Everyone is good at something," said Susu. "Jane and Trevor just haven't discovered their inner elf talents yet."

"Well, they may not have figured out their inner elf talents, but they sure have discovered their inner mischief talents," Andy told his friends. And just like that, everyone's ears started **tingling**.

When an elf's ears tingle, it's always a sign that something exciting and joyful and cheerful is about to happen.

"You're absolutely right, Andy," Susu said excitedly. **"Now let's get to work!"**

The next morning the elves were greeted with a fresh new blanket of snow. "We couldn't have planned this any better," Susu said on the walk to Elf Academy.

The morning went quickly, with three book report **presentations** and a math lesson on fractions.

Luckily, Jane and Trevor didn't pull any **pranks**—for once!

Right before lunch Ms. Dow dismissed class for their morning recess out on the playground, which was covered in mounds and mounds of snow. Andy gathered his friends around and whispered, "Are you ready for Operation Snowball?"

"Ready," they whispered in return, giving a group thumbs-up, and then they split into two teams. When Jane and Trevor came outside, Jay called to Jane to join their team, and Zahara shouted to Trevor to join theirs.

Andy scooped up a handful of snow, packed it into a ball, and let it fly.

"Let the games begin!" he yelled, and . . .

Zip!

Zip!

Zap!

Snowballs flew from one end of the playground to the other . . . smushing slides, smacking swings,

and slamming seesaws and every elf in sight.

This is awesome, Andy thought as he watched the epic fight. *I hope Jane and Trevor think so too.*

"Super shot, Jane," Nicole said as a snowball plopped onto the top of Andy's cap.

"Great **aim**," Andy told Trevor when he managed to knock a hat off a snowman across the playground.

Trevor smiled and replied,

"Thanks, Andy." But then Trevor put down the snowball he was holding and waved Jane over to join them. "Andy, Jane and I owe you and your friends an apology," he began, "for all the tricks we played on everyone."

He paused and then continued, "We didn't mean any harm, but we wanted to be the only elves left to be picked for Elf of the Week. We were so worried no one would want to be friends with us unless we were super elves like you all are."

"We hope we didn't get you into too much trouble," Jane added.

Now Andy was the one to smile. "Oh, I'm used to that," he laughed. "But we would have been your friends no matter what. It might look like we're super elves, but we've lived here and gone to Elf Academy for a long time. There's always time to learn and always something new to learn."

"And what we're about to learn

any second is that if we don't start throwing snowballs again, we're going to get creamed!" Andy shouted.

Trevor picked up three snowballs, shouted, **"Watch this!"** and threw them with all his might. And . . .

Zip!

Zip!

Splat!

He watched as they sailed past
Jay, Nicole, Susu, Zahara, and Kal
and...just missed Ms. Dow's head!
"Oh, no, no, no!" screamed
Trevor.

Ms. Dow looked up into the

open-mouthed faces of her class.

"Recess is over," she said
sternly. "Back to class, now."

Once they were inside at their
workstations, the elves sat quietly.
Ms. Dow stood at the front of the
class, not looking one bit happy.

Ms. Dow began, "I know that
when it snows, it's always fun to
have a snowball fight. However,
today's event was not **scheduled**

or planned. And as you all saw, snow was flying every which way."

She paused, and then added, "As a result, no one will be chosen for Elf of the Week."

Andy turned to look at his friends, and they were all smiling, especially Jane and Trevor.

"Do you mean it, Ms. Dow?" Andy asked. "No elf is more super than another?"

"I wouldn't exactly put it that way, Andy," she answered. "But in a manner of speaking, yes."

"That's just what we thought," Andy said. **"All elves are super elves!"**

And Andy was sure at that very moment that everyone's ears started to tingle!

Word List

aim (AYM): Ability to hit a target

amphibian (am•FIB•ee•uhn): A small animal that lives part of its life cycle in water and part on land

basics (BAY•sihks): Things that serve as the starting point

disruptive (diss•RUHP•tihv): Causing problems

escaped (eh•SKAYPT): Failed to be noticed by

favor (FAY•ver): A kind act

fir (FUR): A type of evergreen tree

gestured (jes•CHURD): Moved one's body to express an idea

knowledgeable (NAH•lih•juh•buhl): Having information

munching (MUHN•ching): Snacking

nervous (NUR•vuss): Uneasy

powdery (POW•duh•ree): Made up of fine, very small pieces

pranks (PRANX): Mischievous tricks

presentations (pree•zen•TAY•shuns): Statements describing or explaining something

recovered (rih•KUH•verd): Reached a normal condition again

relief (rih•LEEF): Removal of something painful or upsetting

remind (rih•MIND): Cause to remember

scheduled (SKED•juhld): Planned when events will happen

scoop (SKOOP): Pick up quickly

slimy (SLY•mee): Slippery and thick or sticky

sternly (STURN•lee): Harshly

swatting (SWAH•ting): Hitting something away

tingling (TING•gling): Feeling a stinging, prickling, or thrilling sensation

Questions

1. Why did Jane and Trevor want to become Elf of the Week?
2. Who was the five-time Annual Snowball Fight champion?
3. Which are you better at building—snow animals or snow people?
4. Why do you think Principal Evergreen didn't like the cookies?
5. Have you ever had to start at a new school or somewhere else

where you had to make new friends?

5. When do elves' ears tingle?

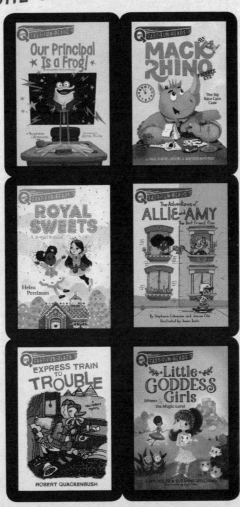